皮皮與波西

♥IREAD

皮皮與波西：新朋友

繪　　圖	阿克賽爾・薛弗勒
譯　　者	酪梨壽司
發 行 人	劉振強
出 版 者	三民書局股份有限公司
地　　址	臺北市復興北路 386 號 (復北門市)
	臺北市重慶南路一段 61 號 (重南門市)
電　　話	(02)25006600
網　　址	三民網路書店 https://www.sanmin.com.tw
出版日期	初版一刷 2019 年 1 月
	初版三刷 2022 年 3 月
書籍編號	S858190
Ｉ Ｓ Ｂ Ｎ	978-957-14-6538-8

Originally published in the English language as
PIP AND POSY: THE NEW FRIEND
Text Copyright © Nosy Crow Ltd 2016
Illustration Copyright © Axel Scheffler 2016
Copyright licensed by Nosy Crow Ltd.
Chinese translation right © 2016 San Min Book Co., Ltd.

小山丘官網

皮皮與波西

新朋友

阿克賽爾·薛弗勒／圖　　酪梨壽司／譯

小山丘　　nosy crow

皮ㄆㄧˊ皮ㄆㄧˊ和ㄏㄜˊ波ㄅㄛ西ㄒㄧ一ㄧˋ起ㄑㄧˇ去ㄑㄩˋ海ㄏㄞˇ邊ㄅㄧㄢ玩ㄨㄢˊ。

他們拿出所有的海灘裝備。

波西提醒：
「別忘了戴遮陽帽喔，皮皮。」

他們一起撿貝殼。

他們在沙灘上挖洞。

他（ㄊㄚ）們（ㄇㄣ）還（ㄏㄞ）光（ㄍㄨㄤ）著（ㄓㄜ）腳（ㄐㄧㄠ）丫（ㄧㄚ）踩（ㄘㄞ）浪（ㄌㄤ）花（ㄏㄨㄚ）。

波西玩累了，小睡一下。

就在這時候，皮皮注意到旁邊有個男孩。

「我ㄨㄛˇ叫ㄐㄧㄠˋ札ㄓㄚˊ克ㄎㄜˋ，我ㄨㄛˇ們ㄇㄣ˙一ㄧ起ㄑㄧˇ玩ㄨㄢˊ好ㄏㄠˇ嗎ㄇㄚ˙？」
男ㄋㄢˊ孩ㄏㄞˊ問ㄨㄣˋ。

「好ㄏㄠˇ啊ㄚ˙，一ㄧ起ㄑㄧˇ玩ㄨㄢˊ！」皮ㄆㄧˊ皮ㄆㄧˊ回ㄏㄨㄟˊ答ㄉㄚˊ。

札_{ㄓㄚˊ}克_{ㄎㄜˋ}和_{ㄏㄢ}皮_{ㄆㄧˊ}皮_{ㄆㄧˊ}一_一起_{ㄑㄧˇ}玩_{ㄨㄢˊ}沙_{ㄕㄚ}灘_{ㄊㄢ}球_{ㄑㄧㄡˊ}。

他_{ㄊㄚ}們_{ㄇㄣˊ}比_{ㄅㄧˇ}賽_{ㄙㄞˋ}倒_{ㄉㄠˋ}立_{ㄌㄧˋ}。

札_{ㄓㄚˊ}克_{ㄎㄜˋ}超_{ㄔㄠ}厲_{ㄌㄧˋ}害_{ㄏㄞˋ}！

札克甚至讓皮皮
試戴他的蛙鏡，試穿他的蛙鞋。

皮皮和札克笑得太大聲，
把波西吵醒了。

「快來跟我們一起玩啊，波西！」皮皮說。

但波西不喜歡札克和皮皮玩的遊戲。

她覺得自己被冷落了。

這時，札克提議去買冰淇淋。

波西說她也要跟。

然而，當他們付錢的時候，
不幸的事發生了。

一隻海鷗飛過來，搶走了札克的冰淇淋！

札ㄚˊ克ㄜˋ非ㄈㄟ常ㄔㄤˊ非ㄈㄟ常ㄔㄤˊ傷ㄕㄤ心ㄒㄧㄣ。

可ㄎㄜˇ憐ㄌㄧㄢˊ的ㄉㄜ札ㄚˊ克ㄜˋ！

這時，波西有個好點子。
她把身上最後一個銅板給札克，
讓他再買一支冰淇淋。

「謝謝妳，波西！」札克抽抽噎噎的說。

皮皮、波西和札克帶著新買的冰淇淋，
沿著海灘走回去。

「接下來妳想玩什麼，波西？」
皮皮問。

波(ㄅㄛ)西(ㄒㄧ)覺(ㄐㄩㄝ)得(ㄉㄜ)他(ㄊㄚ)們(ㄇㄣ)應(ㄧㄥ)該(ㄍㄞ)合(ㄏㄜ)力(ㄌㄧ)堆(ㄉㄨㄟ)一(ㄧ)座(ㄗㄨㄛ)巨(ㄐㄩ)大(ㄉㄚ)的(ㄉㄜ)沙(ㄕㄚ)堡(ㄅㄠ)。

大ㄉㄚˋ功ㄍㄨㄥ告ㄍㄠˋ成ㄔㄥˊ！

太ㄊㄞˋ棒ㄅㄤˋ啦ㄌㄚ！

Pip and Posy were
going to the beach.

They unpacked their things.

"Don't forget to wear your
sun hat, Pip," said Posy.

They collected shells.

They dug a little hole.

And they paddled in the sea.

After that, Posy had a nap.

Just then, Pip noticed a boy next to them.

"I'm Zac," said the boy.
"Would you like to play with me?"

"Yes, please," said Pip.

Zac and Pip played with the beach ball.

They did handstands.

Zac was really good at it!

Zac even let Pip try on
his goggles and flippers.

Pip and Zac were laughing so much
that they woke Posy up.

"Come and play with us, Posy!" said Pip.

But Posy didn't like Zac and Pip's games.

She felt left out.

Then, Zac said that they should go and buy ice creams.

But, as they were paying their money, a bad thing happened.

Posy said she would come, too.

A seagull came and **stole** Zac's ice cream!

Oh dear!

Zac was **very** sad, indeed.

Poor Zac!

Then Posy had a good idea.
She gave Zac her last coin so he
could buy himself a new ice cream.

"Thank you, Posy" sniffed Zac.

Pip, Posy and Zac walked back along the beach with the new ice cream.

"What game would you like to play next, Posy?" said Pip.

Posy thought that they should all build a huge sandcastle.

So that's what they did.

Hooray!

阿克賽爾・薛弗勒　Axel Scheffler

1957年出生於德國漢堡市，25歲時前往英國就讀巴斯藝術學院。他的插畫風格幽默又不失優雅，最著名的當屬《古飛樂》(Gruffalo) 系列作品，不僅榮獲英國多項繪本大獎，譯作超過40種語言，還曾改編為動畫，深受全球觀眾喜愛，是世界知名的繪本作家。

薛弗勒現居英國，持續創作中。

酪梨壽司

當過記者、玩過行銷，在紐約和東京流浪多年後，終於返鄉定居的臺灣媽媽。出沒於臉書專頁「酪梨壽司」與個人部落格「酪梨壽司的日記」。